WHERE LILY ISN'T

Julie Paschkis

illustrations by

Margaret Chodos-Irvine

Henry Holt and Company · New York

Henry Holt and Company, *Publishers since 1866*
Henry Holt® is a registered trademark of Macmillan Publishing Group, LLC
120 Broadway, New York, NY 10271 • mackids.com

Library of Congress Control Number: 2019941050
ISBN 978-1-250-18425-2

Our books may be purchased in bulk for promotional, educational, or business use.
Please contact your local bookseller or the Macmillan Corporate and Premium Sales Department at
(800) 221-7945 ext. 5442 or by email at MacmillanSpecialMarkets@macmillan.com.

First edition, 2020 / Design by Liz Dresner
The artist used hand-cut stencils and gouache on Bristol board to create these illustrations.
Printed in China by Toppan Leefung Printing Ltd.,
Dongguan City, Guangdong Province
1 3 5 7 9 10 8 6 4 2

Dedicated to
Stanley, Boo, Stinker,
Freya, Bluey, Ajax,
and Lily

Lily ran

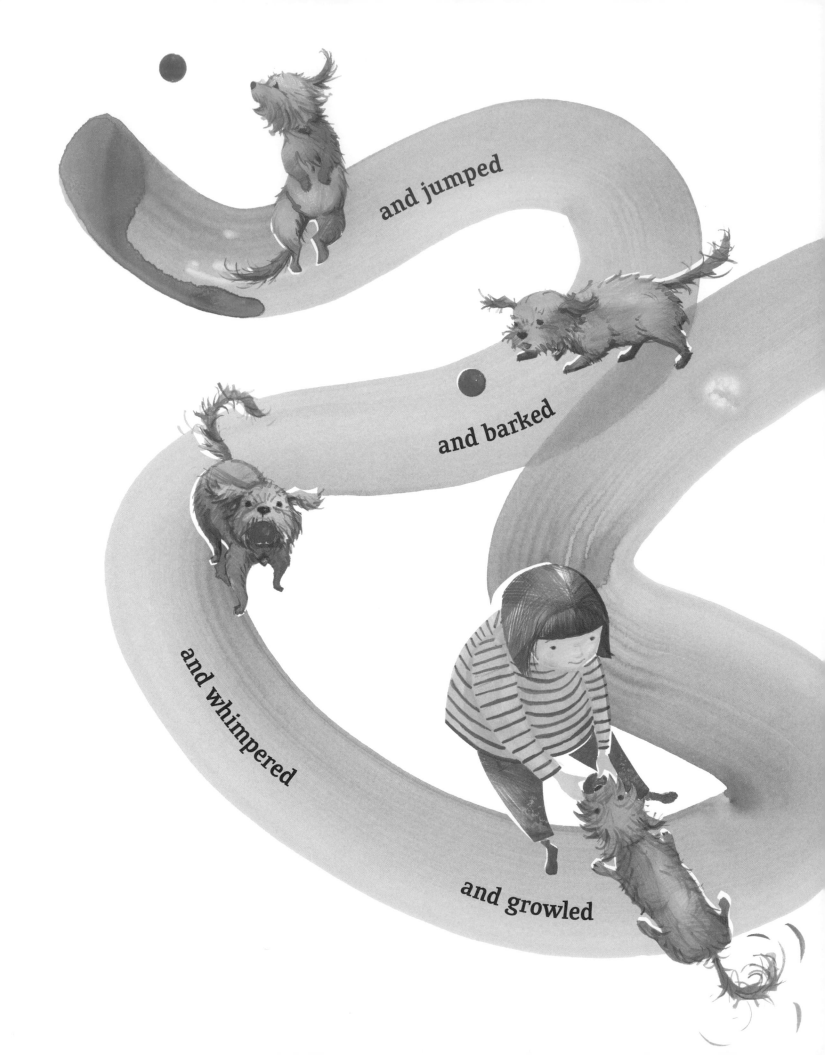

and jumped

and barked

and whimpered

and growled

and wiggled

and wagged

and licked

and snuggled.

But not now.

Now, next to my bed
in the morning,

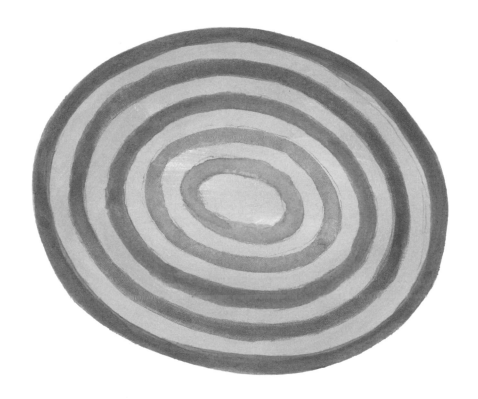

there is a little rug
where Lily isn't.

Now, when I eat
breakfast,

Lily isn't beside
my chair, waiting
for some food
to fall.

When the mailman comes,

Lily isn't barking at him.

When I draw at the table,

Lily isn't underneath,
pressed against my feet.

When I put on my coat
to go outside,

Lily isn't
jumping up,

jiggling,

ready to go.

When I walk to the park,

Lily isn't pulling me forward

or holding me back.

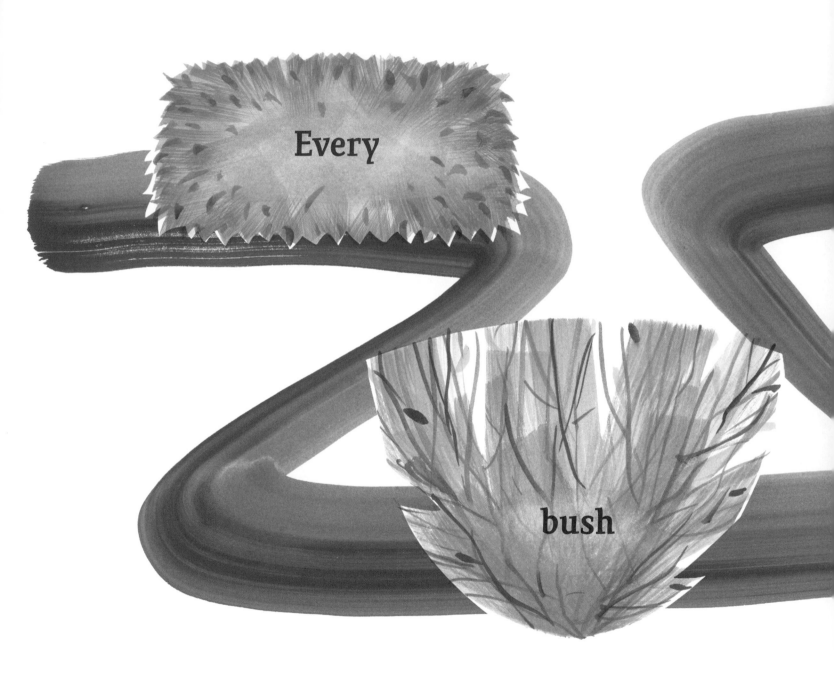

Every

bush

is un- sniffed.

Especially when I come home from school,

Lily isn't there,
waiting just inside
the door.

She isn't there to bark hello
or lick my hand
or snuggle.

There is no belly to
be rubbed or ears
to be scratched.

The house is quiet
with all the sounds
that Lily isn't making.

The house is full of
all the places where
Lily isn't.

But here inside me—

that's where Lily is,

and where she always will be.